empty to enough

courtney n. williams

www.capturingletters.com

contents

Have you ever struggled to put words to your feelings?
Do you feel empty or misunderstood? Are you tired
of surface conversations? Do you need to hold on
to something real? Join me on a journey from empty
to enough. Let these words soak into your soul and
inspire you. Discover something new about yourself.
Gain a better insight into your feelings...your pain, your
heartache, your joy, your hope. Realize that, ultimately,
He is enough.

Words encourage you to feel, think, remember, forget.
The common becomes extraordinary.
The simple, complex.
Sentences sweep you away from the mundane out
to the ocean of possibility.
You can drown. You can float. You can soar.

But, when the eternal powers the pen like a
lightning bolt from the heavenly heights,
Spirit soaked words appear.
No longer anchored to the earth,
something uncontainable happens.

You can't be unwelcome here.

Come and see. Slowly soak in His sovereignty.

Be still and let these words wreck you, challenge you,

pierce a tiny hole in your ordinary so He can work.

Or just breeze by. You get to choose.

But you can't be un**welcome** here.

empty.

endure.

evaluate.

emerge.

enough.

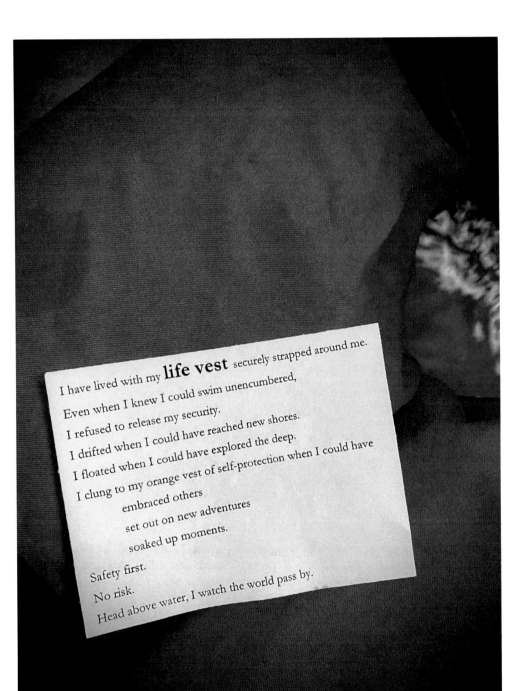

I have lived with my **life vest** securely strapped around me.

Even when I knew I could swim unencumbered,

I refused to release my security.

I drifted when I could have reached new shores.

I floated when I could have explored the deep.

I clung to my orange vest of self-protection when I could have

       embraced others

       set out on new adventures

       soaked up moments.

Safety first.

No risk.

Head above water, I watch the world pass by.

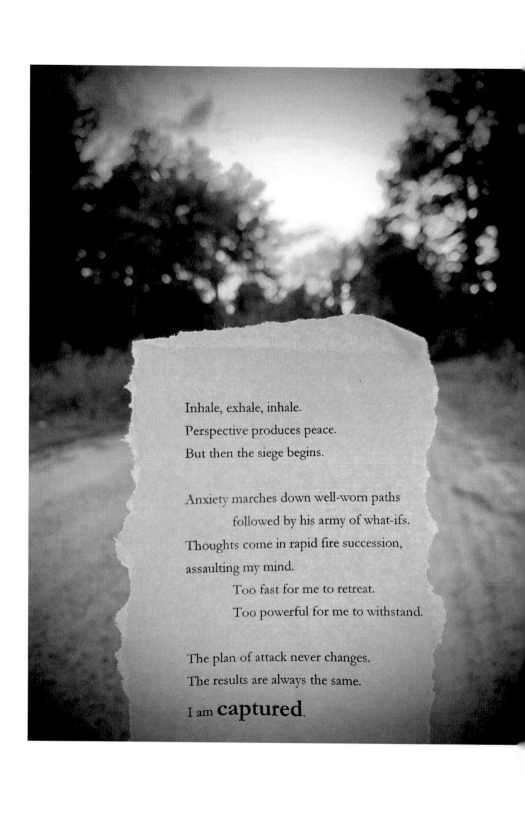

Inhale, exhale, inhale.
Perspective produces peace.
But then the siege begins.

Anxiety marches down well-worn paths
	followed by his army of what-ifs.
Thoughts come in rapid fire succession,
assaulting my mind.
		Too fast for me to retreat.
		Too powerful for me to withstand.

The plan of attack never changes.
The results are always the same.
I am **captured**.

The **pull**

of internal conflict

stretches me

tears me

empties me

until I am no longer whole.

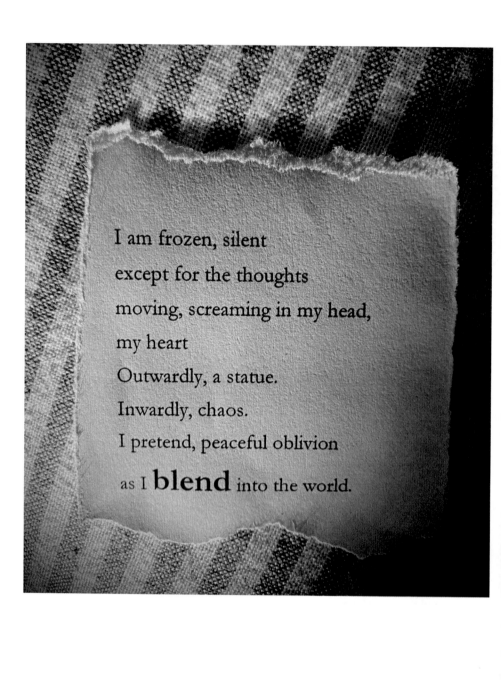

I am frozen, silent
except for the thoughts
moving, screaming in my head,
my heart
Outwardly, a statue.
Inwardly, chaos.
I pretend, peaceful oblivion
as I **blend** into the world.

There is something broken down deep inside me
so far beneath the me I know that it is difficult to identify,
but I can feel the weight of the damage.

When was the moment I adopted the idea
I wasn't good enough...
I had to conform to survive?
That second, lost in time, triggered an earthquake
inside me
of such a great magnitude
that all that was stable and secure
ruptured.

Deep ruts and ridges ripped through me,
altering His design.
Individuality and Confidence tumbled into these massive fissures
and remain buried beneath the rubble.
How will I pull them out, rescue them...

rescue me?

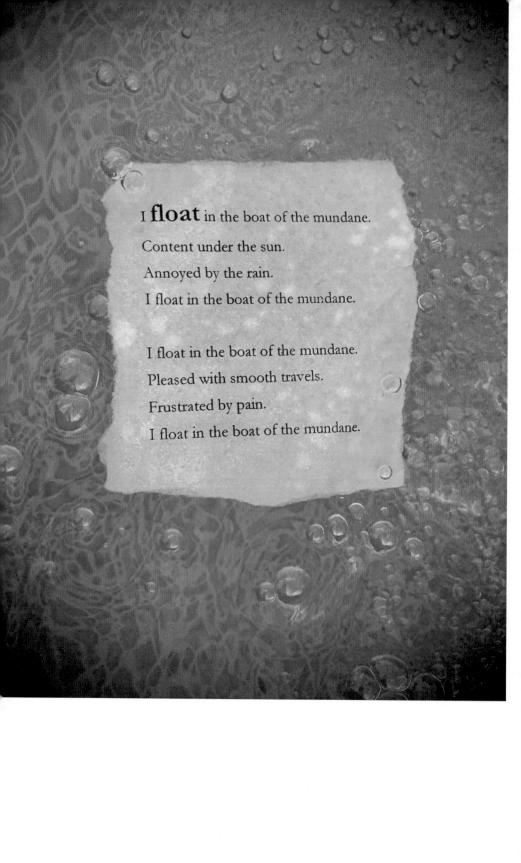

I **float** in the boat of the mundane.

Content under the sun.

Annoyed by the rain.

I float in the boat of the mundane.

I float in the boat of the mundane.

Pleased with smooth travels.

Frustrated by pain.

I float in the boat of the mundane.

Nothing seems substantial.
Everything feels weighty.

I breathe.

in.out.in.out.in

The monotony of it.
The power of it,
this air flowing through my lungs.

Without it, I die.
The necessity of it, terrifying.
What if my lungs forget?
What if the air is toxic?
What if….

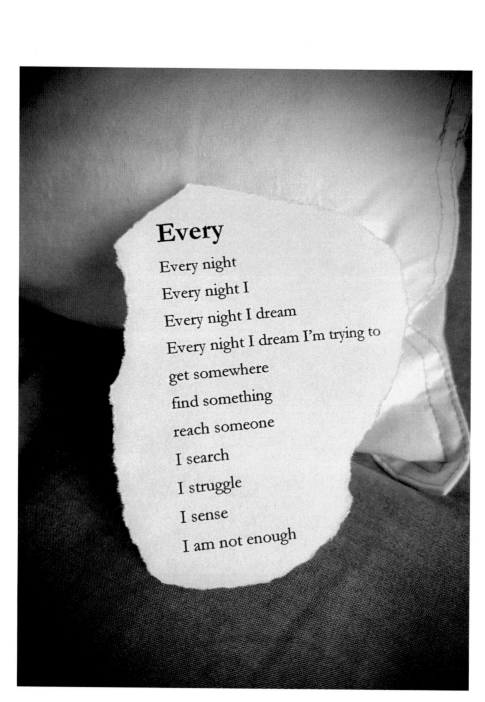

Every

Every night

Every night I

Every night I dream

Every night I dream I'm trying to

get somewhere

find something

reach someone

I search

I struggle

I sense

I am not enough

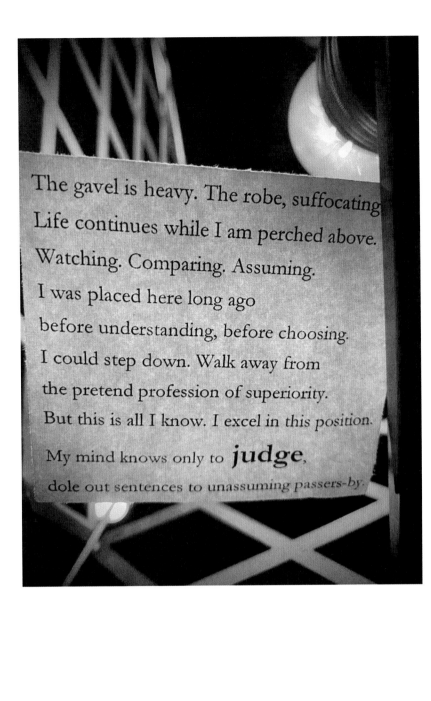

The gavel is heavy. The robe, suffocating.
Life continues while I am perched above.
Watching. Comparing. Assuming.
I was placed here long ago
before understanding, before choosing.
I could step down. Walk away from
the pretend profession of superiority.
But this is all I know. I excel in this position.

My mind knows only to **judge**,

dole out sentences to unassuming passers-by.

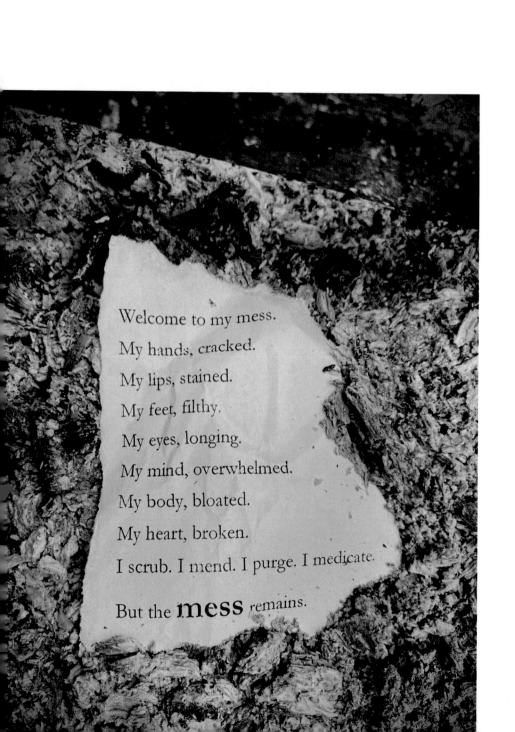

Welcome to my mess.

My hands, cracked.

My lips, stained.

My feet, filthy.

My eyes, longing.

My mind, overwhelmed.

My body, bloated.

My heart, broken.

I scrub. I mend. I purge. I medicate.

But the **mess** remains.

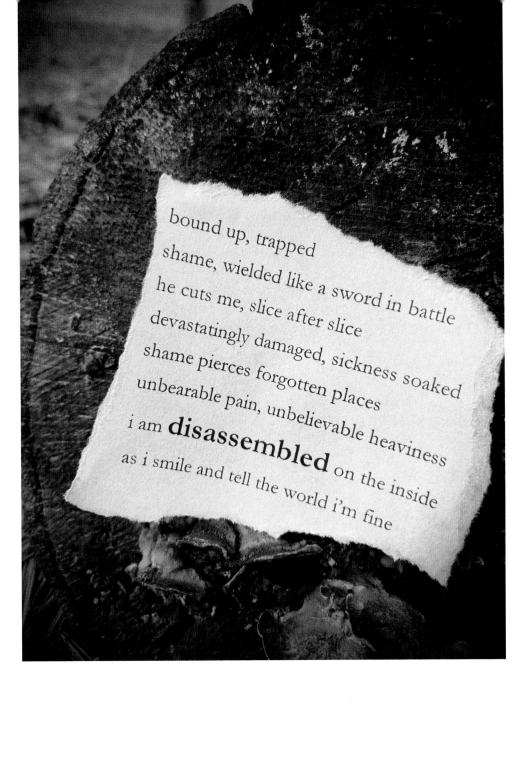

bound up, trapped
shame, wielded like a sword in battle
he cuts me, slice after slice
devastatingly damaged, sickness soaked
shame pierces forgotten places
unbearable pain, unbelievable heaviness
i am **disassembled** on the inside
as i smile and tell the world i'm fine

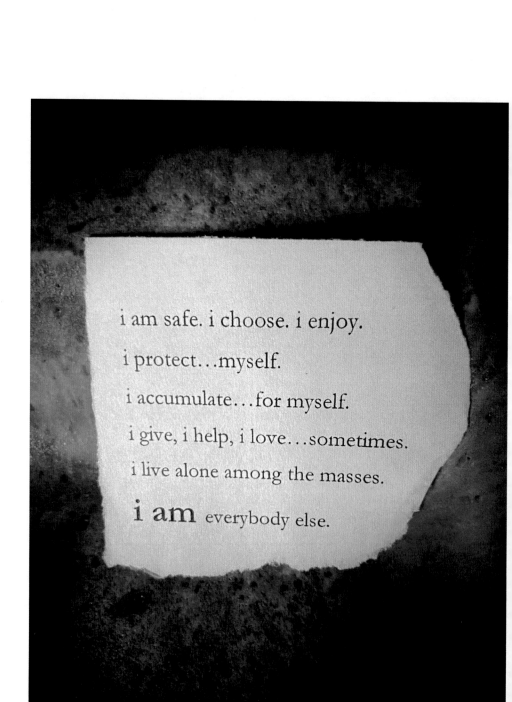

i am safe. i choose. i enjoy.

i protect…myself.

i accumulate…for myself.

i give, i help, i love…sometimes.

i live alone among the masses.

i am everybody else.

empty.

endure.

evaluate.

emerge.

enough.

I bleed from the shards of your **fractured** life.

But you pay no attention.

In your world, there is only you.

You are ruler, master, receiver.

You are blind to the fragments of glass surrounding you.

Sharp.

Painful.

Tinged in red.

Those brave enough to venture close are met with

rough edges, sharp points and poisonous seepage.

But you find comfort in your oblivion.

Keep pretending you are unbroken.

Keep ignoring the carnage in your wake.

And I will keep peeling and pressing the band aids.

The weight of the words you never speak crush me.

Tell me I am loved.

Tell me I am wanted.

Tell me I am enough.

Eyes, searching. Ears, straining. Heart, breaking.

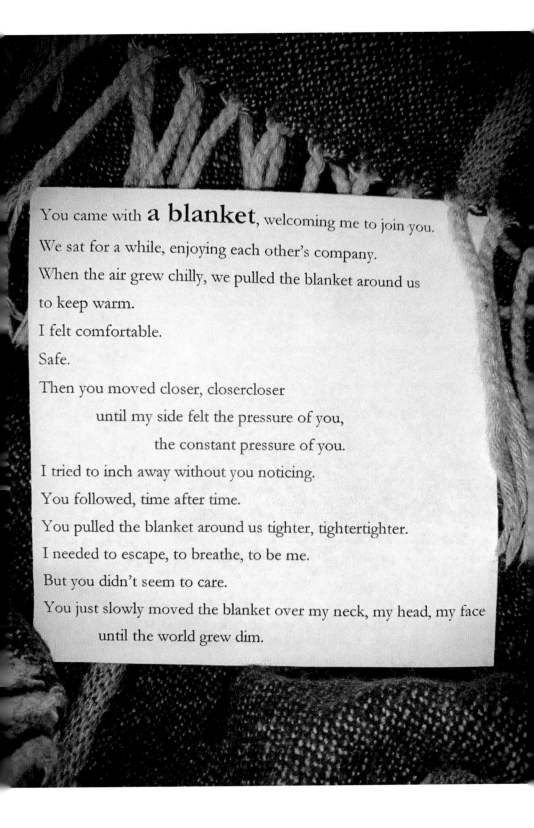

You came with **a blanket**, welcoming me to join you.

We sat for a while, enjoying each other's company.

When the air grew chilly, we pulled the blanket around us
to keep warm.

I felt comfortable.

Safe.

Then you moved closer, closercloser
       until my side felt the pressure of you,
           the constant pressure of you.

I tried to inch away without you noticing.

You followed, time after time.

You pulled the blanket around us tighter, tightertighter.

I needed to escape, to breathe, to be me.

But you didn't seem to care.

You just slowly moved the blanket over my neck, my head, my face
       until the world grew dim.

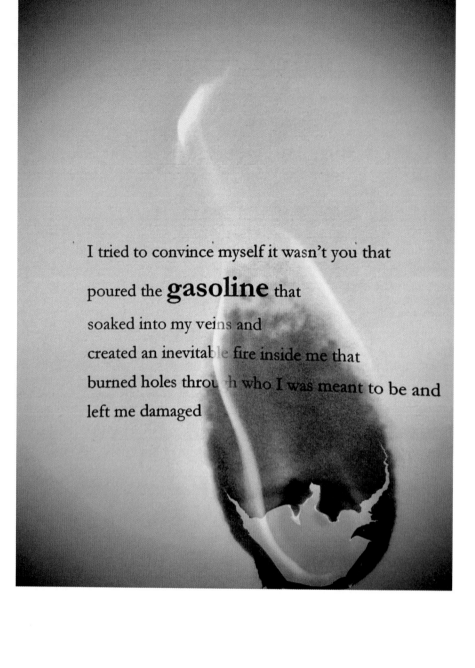

I tried to convince myself it wasn't you that

poured the **gasoline** that

soaked into my veins and

created an inevitable fire inside me that

burned holes through who I was meant to be and

left me damaged

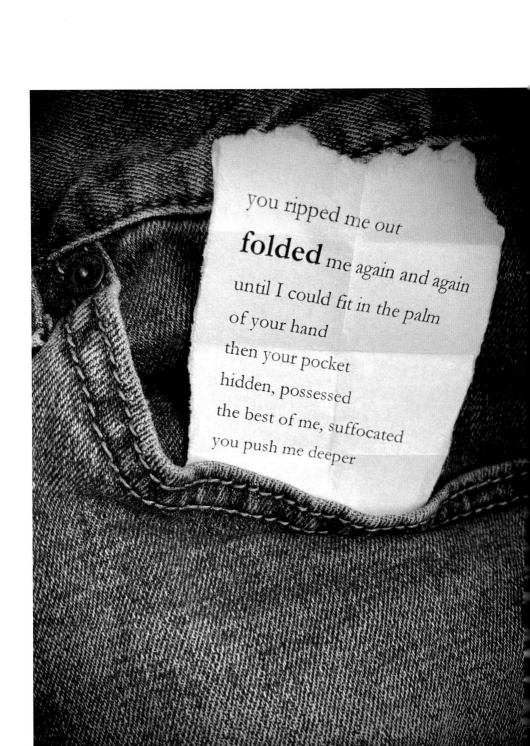

you ripped me out
folded me again and again
until I could fit in the palm
of your hand
then your pocket
hidden, possessed
the best of me, suffocated
you push me deeper

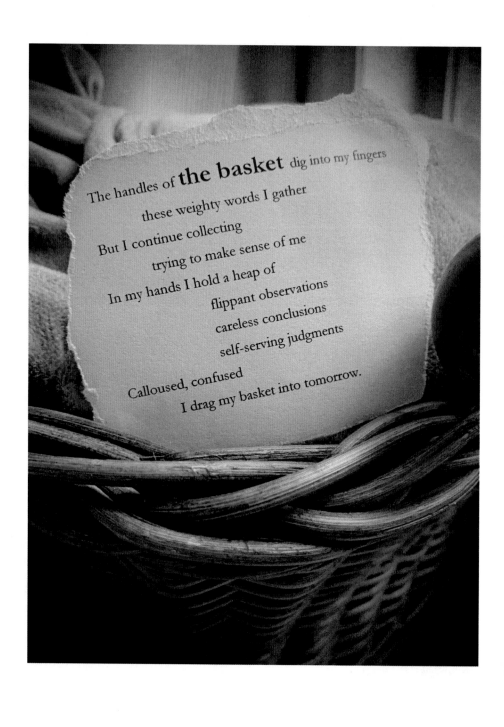

The handles of **the basket** dig into my fingers
these weighty words I gather
But I continue collecting
trying to make sense of me
In my hands I hold a heap of
flippant observations
careless conclusions
self-serving judgments

Calloused, confused
I drag my basket into tomorrow.

I have worn my **mask** for so long

that I am unsure of what is underneath

and why I was taught to wear it in the first place.

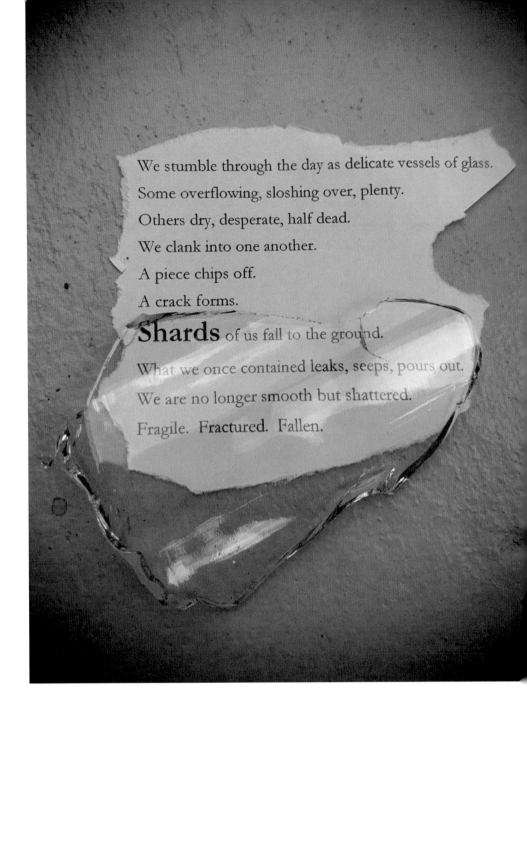

We stumble through the day as delicate vessels of glass.

Some overflowing, sloshing over, plenty.

Others dry, desperate, half dead.

We clank into one another.

A piece chips off.

A crack forms.

Shards of us fall to the ground.

What we once contained leaks, seeps, pours out.

We are no longer smooth but shattered.

Fragile. Fractured. Fallen.

the **wounds** you inflict

bruise my confidence

scar my joy

puncture my peace

break my heart

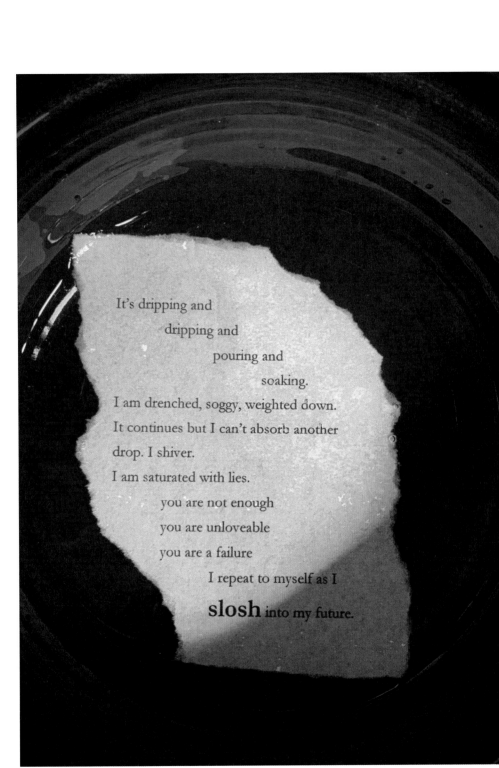

It's dripping and
          dripping and
                    pouring and
                              soaking.
I am drenched, soggy, weighted down.
It continues but I can't absorb another
drop. I shiver.
I am saturated with lies.
          you are not enough
          you are unloveable
          you are a failure
                    I repeat to myself as I
          slosh into my future.

empty.

endure.

evaluate.

emerge.

enough.

tilt it over
shift it slightly
move it around

look from a different **angle**
stop skimming over the familiar
dig in slowly

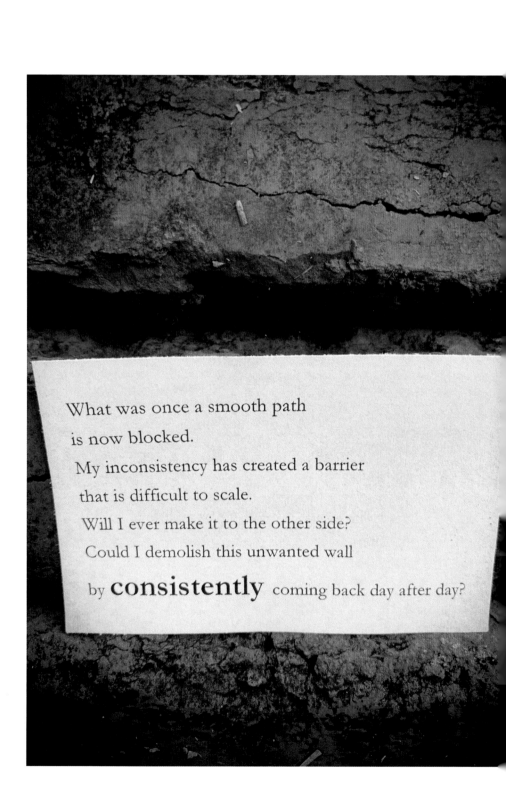

What was once a smooth path

is now blocked.

My inconsistency has created a barrier

that is difficult to scale.

Will I ever make it to the other side?

Could I demolish this unwanted wall

by **consistently** coming back day after day?

I allowed the years to **manipulate** the past. Situations reassembled themselves in my mind until I began to wonder if I was even there at all

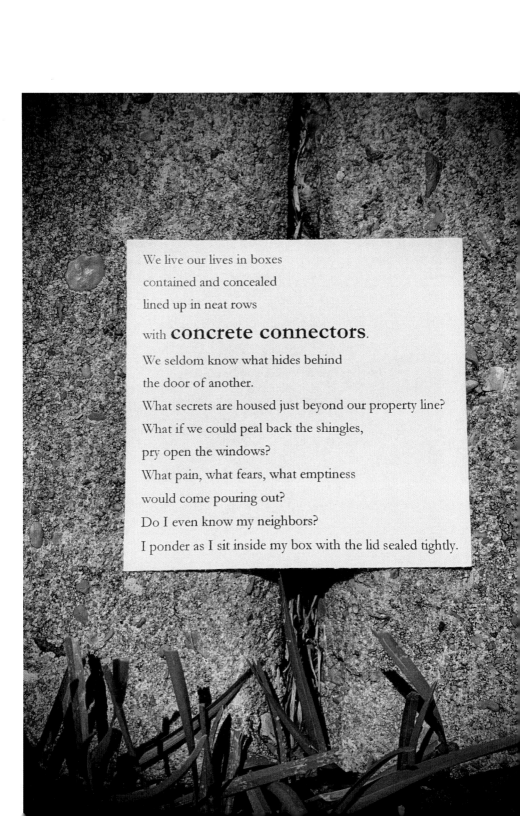

We live our lives in boxes

contained and concealed

lined up in neat rows

with **concrete connectors**.

We seldom know what hides behind

the door of another.

What secrets are housed just beyond our property line?

What if we could peal back the shingles,

pry open the windows?

What pain, what fears, what emptiness

would come pouring out?

Do I even know my neighbors?

I ponder as I sit inside my box with the lid sealed tightly.

how did the minutes

    slip

        so quickly

between

        my fingers?

have i really had so much time?

so slippery.

so delicate.

the **hours**

    crash

        to the ground

and i am left

    older

    standing still

    waiting…

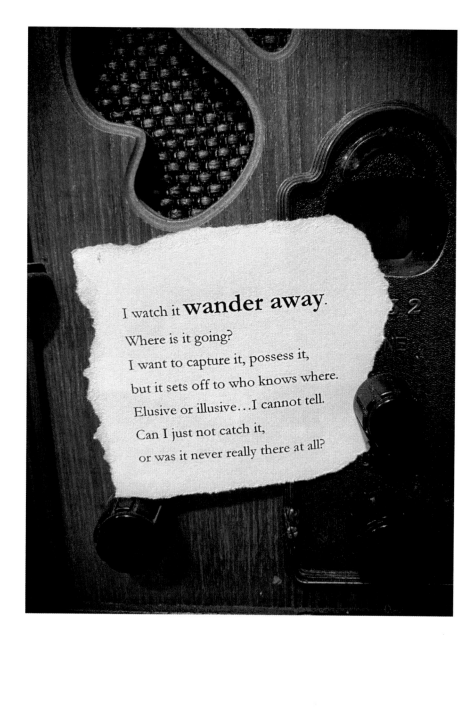

I watch it **wander away**.

Where is it going?

I want to capture it, possess it,

but it sets off to who knows where.

Elusive or illusive…I cannot tell.

Can I just not catch it,

or was it never really there at all?

my eyes have grown wild
searching to see
darkness has settled
but i know He is there
the realm of the Spirit
just beyond my reach

i failed to simply **ask**

Eyelids close.

World fades.

Surroundings shut out.

Focus on Him.

Sight, illuminated.

Hearing, inaudible.

Communication, inexplicable.

Do you truly see with open eyes?

Opposition. Battle lines are drawn.
I just want both sides to compromise
to blur the line, to meet in the middle
no winner, no loser, just harmony.
But it will never be.
The two factions are diametrically opposed.

                I stand in the middle.
He stands on one side; the world, the other.
All authority, power, hope, future vs
everything temporary, finite, normal, now.
One side whispers, tugs; the other screams, lures.
Death and destruction against life and prosperity.
The choice, obvious. The challenge, overwhelming.

I declared my allegiance long ago.
Saved. Chosen. Cleansed.
But the other side remains
fighting for parts of me.
Instead of joining my Leader
I keep returning to neutral ground
where I think
                I am the center.
But here I am
                exposed
                conflicted
                undone

        TRAITOR.

The living, active Word of God
   forgotten on a shelf
   set out for display
   tossed on the back seat
   left to collect dust
The living, active Word of God
   treated like it is any other book, decoration, clutter.
What if one day…

What if one day the words vanished and the pages were blank
   stark white nothingness
   page after page?
Would you even care?

Would you even **notice**?

empty.

endure.

evaluate.

emerge.

enough.

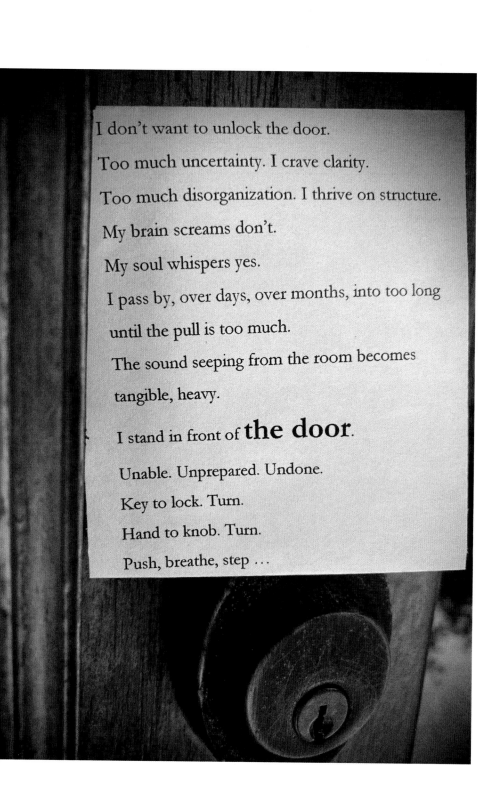

I don't want to unlock the door.

Too much uncertainty. I crave clarity.

Too much disorganization. I thrive on structure.

My brain screams don't.

My soul whispers yes.

I pass by, over days, over months, into too long

until the pull is too much.

The sound seeping from the room becomes

tangible, heavy.

I stand in front of **the door**.

Unable. Unprepared. Undone.

Key to lock. Turn.

Hand to knob. Turn.

Push, breathe, step …

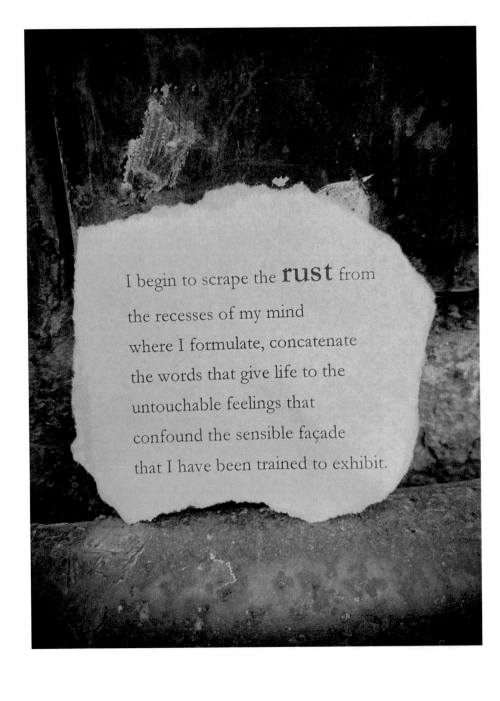

I begin to scrape the rust from
the recesses of my mind
where I formulate, concatenate
the words that give life to the
untouchable feelings that
confound the sensible façade
that I have been trained to exhibit.

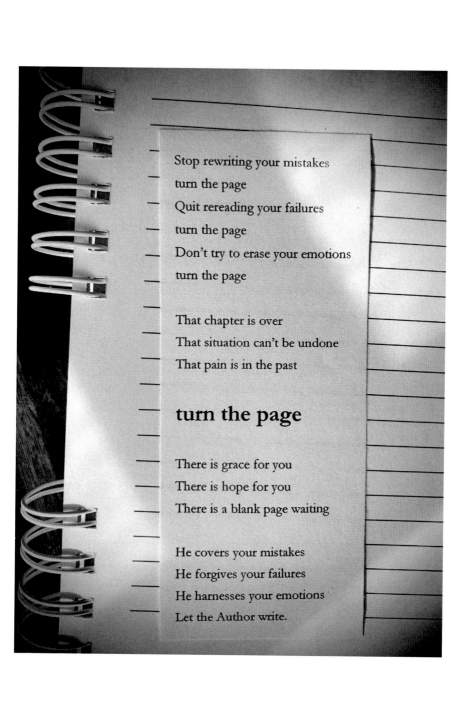

Stop rewriting your mistakes
turn the page
Quit rereading your failures
turn the page
Don't try to erase your emotions
turn the page

That chapter is over
That situation can't be undone
That pain is in the past

turn the page

There is grace for you
There is hope for you
There is a blank page waiting

He covers your mistakes
He forgives your failures
He harnesses your emotions
Let the Author write.

Finite minds, unable to understand forever.
Sin soaked hearts, unaccustomed to purity.
Limited flesh, incapable of grasping eternal.
Corrupt lips, unqualified to offer unstained worship.

Yet here is where we find ourselves

completely **juxtaposed** against His holiness.

We must believe without understanding.
We must confess in our filthiness.
We must hope as we decay.
We must praise without words.

I clutch the familiar, holding on to all I know, assuming this is my journey, my only option.

My fingers are hurting, my body fatigued, yet I continue to grip with all that is in me.

To let go would be to admit I made mistakes. I got it wrong. I wasted time.

I cling to a life that is dissolving in my hands until there is nothing left to grasp.

As I sit in my nothingness, fists still clutching the air, He picks me up, gently pries open my fingers and places His scarred hands in my own.

It feels sticky between my fingers…

this dream of mine.

Tangible but not substantial.

Messy.

Uncontained.

I leave traces of it everywhere.

But I can't seem to gather it from my own flesh,

to solidify it into something nameable.

Index finger to thumb, I test its consistency.

The tackiness.

The staying power.

I contemplate its substance,

my mind traveling

down unknown paths

 as **the dream** seeps into my skin.

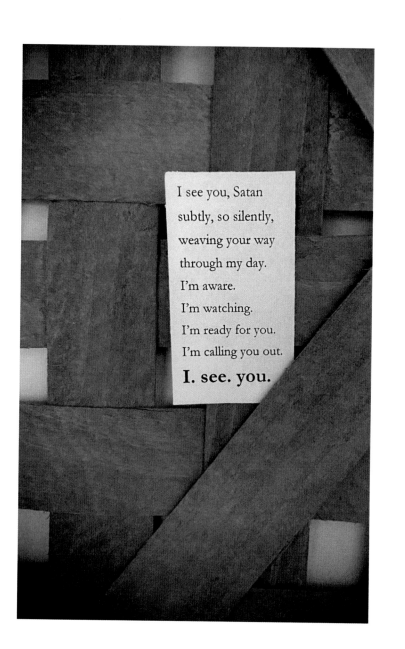

I see you, Satan
subtly, so silently,
weaving your way
through my day.
I'm aware.
I'm watching.
I'm ready for you.
I'm calling you out.

I. see. you.

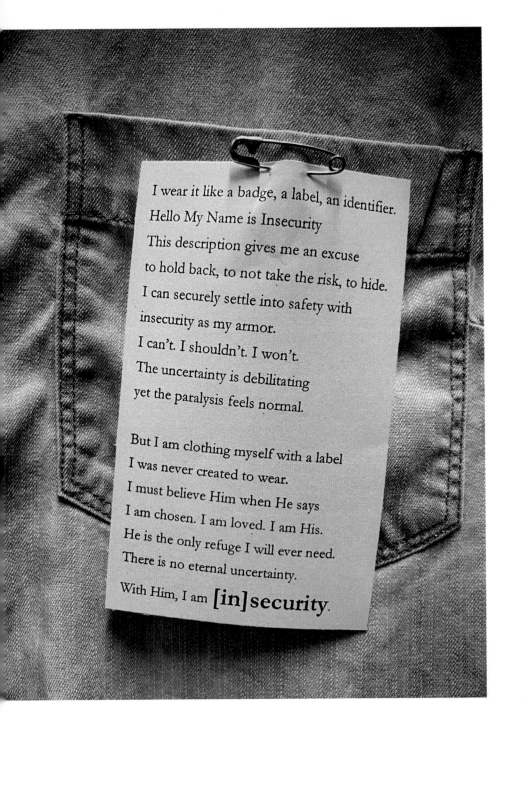

I wear it like a badge, a label, an identifier.
Hello My Name is Insecurity
This description gives me an excuse
to hold back, to not take the risk, to hide.
I can securely settle into safety with
insecurity as my armor.
I can't. I shouldn't. I won't.
The uncertainty is debilitating
yet the paralysis feels normal.

But I am clothing myself with a label
I was never created to wear.
I must believe Him when He says
I am chosen. I am loved. I am His.
He is the only refuge I will ever need.
There is no eternal uncertainty.
With Him, I am [in]security.

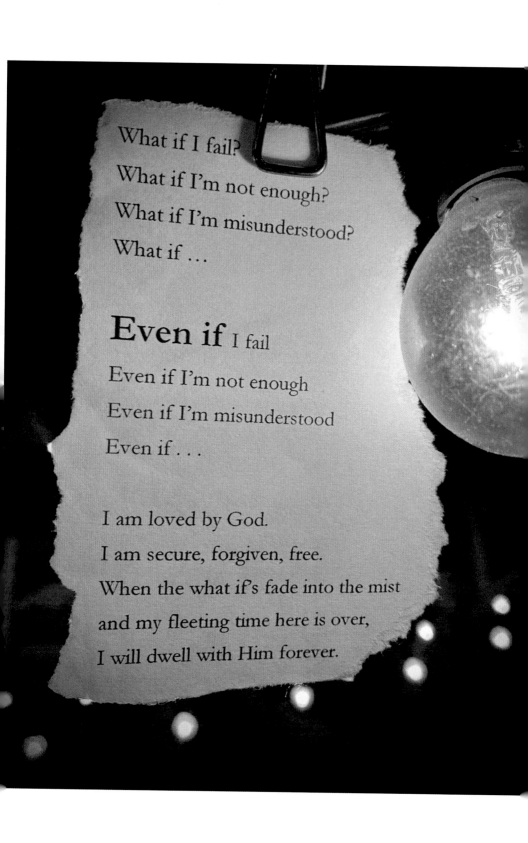

What if I fail?

What if I'm not enough?

What if I'm misunderstood?

What if …

Even if I fail

Even if I'm not enough

Even if I'm misunderstood

Even if …

I am loved by God.

I am secure, forgiven, free.

When the what if's fade into the mist

and my fleeting time here is over,

I will dwell with Him forever.

His Words **wash** me.
over me, through me, into me
until I can see a reflection of Him
in areas no longer stained by self

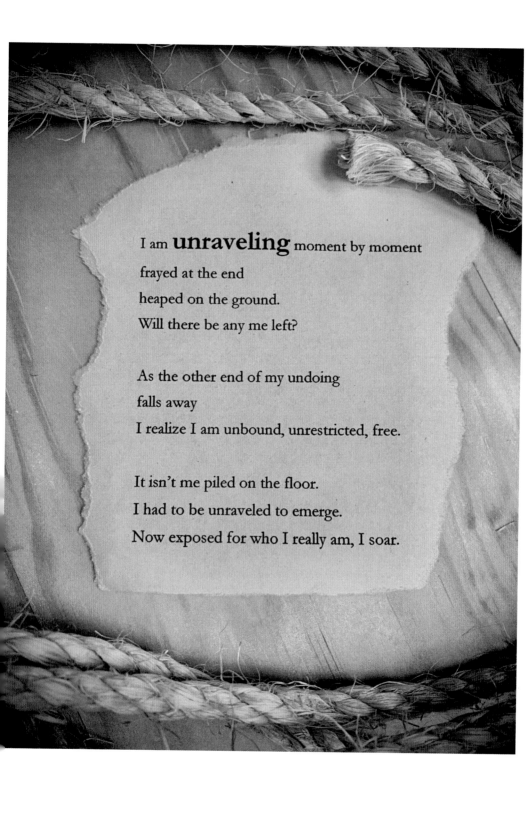

I am **unraveling** moment by moment
frayed at the end
heaped on the ground.
Will there be any me left?

As the other end of my undoing
falls away
I realize I am unbound, unrestricted, free.

It isn't me piled on the floor.
I had to be unraveled to emerge.
Now exposed for who I really am, I soar.

empty.

endure.

evaluate.

emerge.

He is
enough.

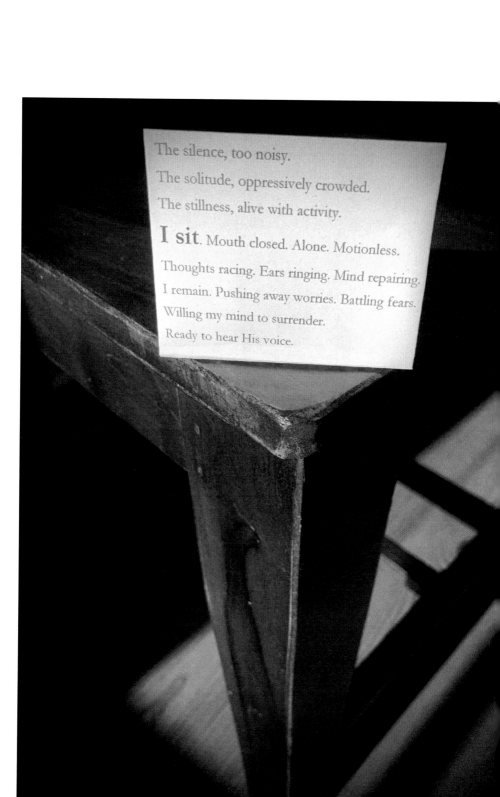

The silence, too noisy.

The solitude, oppressively crowded.

The stillness, alive with activity.

I sit. Mouth closed. Alone. Motionless.

Thoughts racing. Ears ringing. Mind repairing.

I remain. Pushing away worries. Battling fears.

Willing my mind to surrender.

Ready to hear His voice.

Rewind me back to nothingness
Rewind me back to the start
Rewind my failures
Rewind my mistakes
Rewind my tragedy

Rewind me
and unwind until there is only You.

Your life written down in pen. Page after page.

No eraser. No undoing. No ripping.

Each action, each breath, each word is recorded.

We try to smudge away the pain

scribble through mistakes

rip out seasons of sadness.

But all the effort to conceal, to rewrite

changes nothing.

Failures, disappointments, missed opportunities

scream from the pages of you

tainting and overshadowing everything you want to
remember.

But God…

through torn flesh and dark red blood

with nails and jeers

linen and stone

death and resurrection…

He provided an Eraser

to those that call Him, claim Him as their Lord

This supernatural white out covers all that is sinful

throughout the book of you.

He blots out words, paragraphs, whole chapters.

The spaces, the pages, still remain in your story.

The shadow of those missing moments

still remembered at times.

But they aren't you anymore.

They have been erased by the blood of Jesus.

Your life still written down in pen.

Page after page.

But freedom is found in knowing

the **Eraser**.

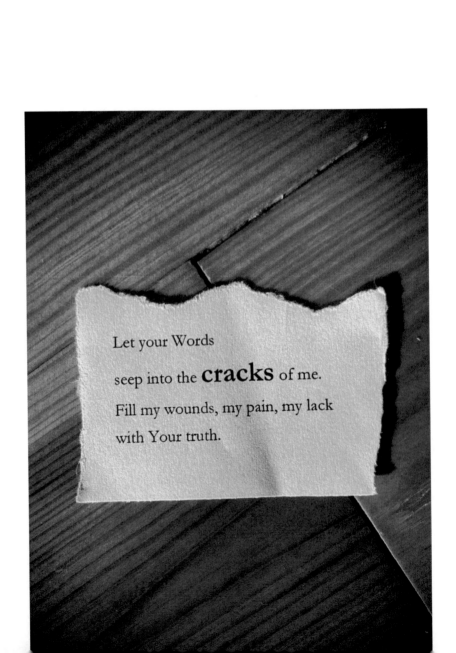

Let your Words

seep into the **cracks** of me.

Fill my wounds, my pain, my lack

with Your truth.

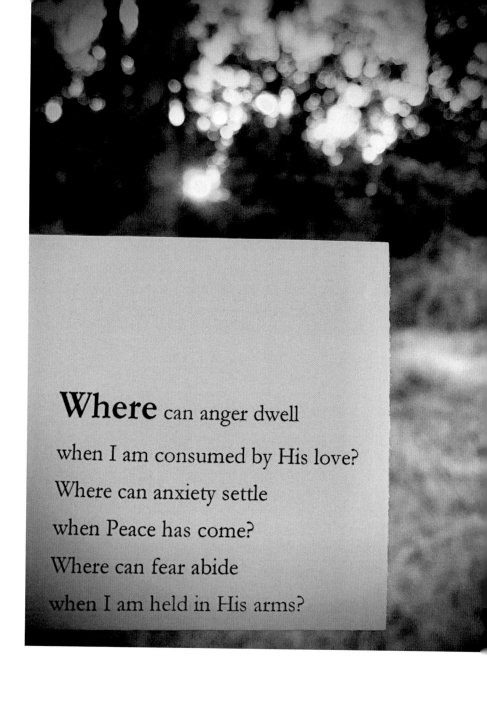

Where can anger dwell
when I am consumed by His love?
Where can anxiety settle
when Peace has come?
Where can fear abide
when I am held in His arms?

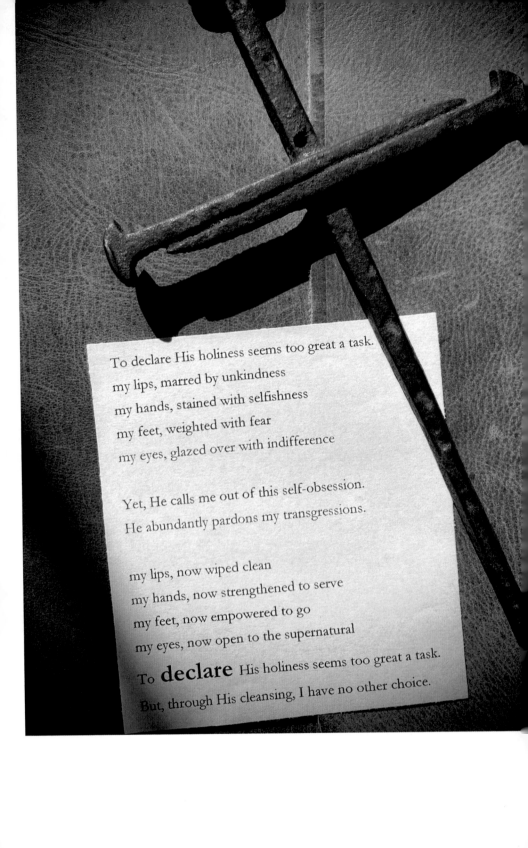

To declare His holiness seems too great a task.

my lips, marred by unkindness
my hands, stained with selfishness
my feet, weighted with fear
my eyes, glazed over with indifference

Yet, He calls me out of this self-obsession.
He abundantly pardons my transgressions.

my lips, now wiped clean
my hands, now strengthened to serve
my feet, now empowered to go
my eyes, now open to the supernatural

To **declare** His holiness seems too great a task.
But, through His cleansing, I have no other choice.

I come before Him
dirty hands, bruised body, head down
broken
        again
suffocating in shame
weighed down with regret
failure
        again
I fall...
I fall before Him because I can do nothing else
He waits...
He waits for me to process
to feel the heaviness of my sin
to grasp the pain I caused
to fear the strength of His wrath
to fully realize that I am hopeless...dead
without Him
I look up...
I look up to His love, His acceptance, His forgiveness
I confess, I apologize, I wait
He pulls...
He pulls me up out of my broken mess
I stand...
I stand before Him, arms out,
handing Him my whole heart
again
His mercy and His grace flow over me
strengthen me, clean me
My filthiness replaced with white
I am made new.

Push over the mountains.

Rewind the wind.

Unbind the ocean.

Write in the clouds.

The world is **Yours**.

The Crucifixion

26 And as they led him away, they seized one Simon of Cyrene, who was coming in from the country, and laid on him the cross, to carry it behind Jesus. **27** And there follow... ...ltitude of the people and of wom... ...nting for him. **28** But...

do no...

29 For l... Stage, set before the foundations of the world.

the ba... Earth, waiting.

never n... King, willing.

on us,' a... People, wanting.

the wood... Wood and nails, whips and evil.

32 Two ...

death with... It's time.

The Skull, ...

right and o... Sword, hurled from heaven

they know ... pierces the ground with open arms.

ments. **35** And... Earth, reverberated.

at him, sayin... King, ransomed.

Christ of God... People, reconciled.

coming up an...

the King of the... Love and hope, peace and forever.

over him, "This...

39 One of the c... "Are you not the... ...us!" **40** But the other rebuked him, say... ...not fear God, since you are under the same sentence of condemnation? **41** And we indeed justly, for we are receiving the due reward of our deeds; but this man has done nothing wrong." **42** And he said, "Jesus, remember me when ...come into your kingdom." **43** And he said to him, "Truly, I say ...today you will be with me in paradise."

Sabbath was beg... from Galilee follo... **56** Then they retu... On the Sabbath...

The Resurrection

24 But on th... the tomb... found the stone... in they did not f... perplexed about... apparel. **5** And as... the ground, the... among the dead... he told you, whi... must be delivere... and on the third... returning from t... and to all the res... ...lary the mothe... ...d these things... ...dle tale, and t... ...e tomb; sto... ...themselves; and...

On the Road to E... **13** That very da... Emmaus, abou... talking with... While th... drew th...

The Words mend me from the inside,

stitching back together

the ripped, the tattered…

piecing together the parts of me

into something less harsh, less fragmented,

more reflective of You.

But what it is about the Words?

Phrases, syllables, letters

birthed out of thought, of experience, of Spirit.

They are not mine to possess.

They belong to You.

Take them up with the wind and

send them out, out into Your creation.

Allow them to be used

to mend others,

to spark thought,

to cause a shift.

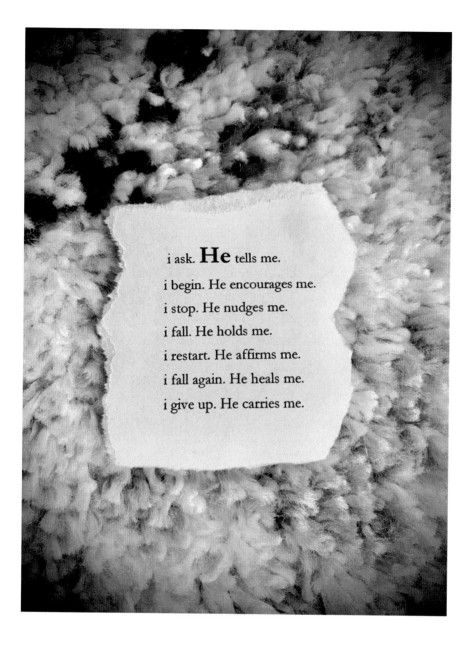

i ask. **He** tells me.

i begin. He encourages me.

i stop. He nudges me.

i fall. He holds me.

i restart. He affirms me.

i fall again. He heals me.

i give up. He carries me.

The mirror screams
you are not enough
Her casual dismissal affirms
you are not enough
Your bank account testifies
you are not enough
His cutting comment confirms
you are not enough
Your secret tears whisper
you are not enough

You strive You search You sacrifice
you are not enough
You love You listen You learn
you are not enough
You compromise You cling You cry
you are not enough

and you never will be
you never can be
you never should be
He must be
He always can be
He always will be
your Enough
only in Him, with Him, through Him
will you be enough
because
He is **Enough**.

He is enough.

Made in the USA
Middletown, DE
22 February 2022

61701389R00042